EYEWITNESS CLASSICS

ROBINSON CRUSOE

A DORLING KINDERSLEY BOOK

ABRIDGED FOR YOUNG READERS

Project Art Editor Mark Regardsoe
Senior Editor Alastair Dougall
Designer Tanya Tween
Research Fergus Day
Production Katy Holmes and Steve Lang
Managing Art Editor Jacquie Gulliver
Picture Research Sean Hunter and Jamie Robinson
DTP Designers Kim Browne and Sarah Williams
Abridgement James Dunbar

First published in Great Britain in 1998 by
Dorling Kindersley Limited, 9 Henrietta Street, London WC2E 8PS

Visit us on the World Wide Web at http://www.dk.com

A CIP catalogue record for this book is available from the British Library.

ISBN 0-7513-7076-2

Colour reproduction by Bright Arts in Hong Kong
Printed by Graphicom in Italy

EYEWITNESS CLASSICS

ROBINSON CRUSOE

DANIEL DEFOE

Illustrated by
JULEK HELLER

DK

DORLING KINDERSLEY

LONDON • NEW YORK • STUTTGART • MOSCOW

CONTENTS

Poll, Crusoe's parrot

Crusoe's dog

Robinson Crusoe

Crusoe's father

The ship's master

Friday

The English captain

INTRODUCTION

Marooned, by Howard Pyle (1909)

THE STORY OF ONE MAN'S BATTLE for survival on a desert island against shipwreck, storms, hunger, and fear, *Robinson Crusoe* is one of the world's greatest and most popular novels of adventure. It has held readers spellbound ever since its publication in 1719, and remains the supreme achievement in the remarkable life of its author, Daniel Defoe.

This *Eyewitness Classic* edition sensitively abridges the original text, simplifying difficult or archaic words and phrases, and including all the book's best-known incidents. Younger readers can thus experience and enjoy the full flavour of the original novel for themselves.

At the same time, the story is firmly set in its historical context. Information pages and fact-and-picture columns reveal Defoe's turbulent times, explain where he found inspiration for his central character, and help to chart Robinson's journeys. They also explore some of the book's fascinating background themes, such as the opening-up of the New World by Europeans, and the hazardous life of a 17th-century sailor. There is also a unique, specially researched map of Crusoe's exotic desert island, based on Defoe's own descriptions.

However, the most fascinating feature of *Robinson Crusoe* remains Robinson himself. As a wild and selfish young man with few skills and less sense, he runs away from his father's humdrum world and finds religious faith and qualities of patience, courage, and endurance he never dreamed he possessed. Turn the pages and become his companion on a thrilling, inspirational, never-to-be-forgotten journey.

NEW WORLD CONQUEST

IN THE 15TH AND 16TH CENTURIES, advances in shipbuilding and navigation led to what must have been an incredible discovery: a vast, unknown continent across the Atlantic. Sailors and soldiers crossed the ocean to explore, conquer, and colonize this land, which they called the New World. Merchants, like Robinson Crusoe, made fortunes by trading with native peoples who were unaware of the value Europeans placed on gold and precious stones. Europeans set up huge plantations to grow sugar, rubber, and cotton. The owners wanted cheap labour, and so the ruthless slave trade was born.

Gérard Depardieu as Columbus in 1492: The Conquest of Paradise (1992).

Columbus Arrives
Attempting to reach Asia by sailing west, Spanish explorer Christopher Columbus discovered the islands of the Caribbean in 1492. He returned with tales of a rich New World.

Conquistadors' helmet

The Conquistadors
By the 1500s, Spanish soldiers equipped with armour, horses, and guns were arriving in Central and South America. The native empires of the Aztecs and Incas were quickly defeated. The Conquistadors, as the soldiers were known, slaughtered thousands, and forcibly converted the survivors to the Catholic religion.

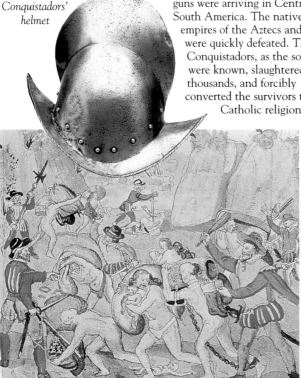

The Massacre of Indians at Cholula, *a watercolour from 1519.*

Tragic mistake
The Aztecs believed that one of their most important gods, the pale-faced Quetzalcoatl, would one day return to them. When the Spanish soldiers first arrived in 1519, they welcomed their leader, Hernán Cortez, as if he was Quetzalcoatl himself.

Ocean crossing
The Spanish and Portuguese were the first great European explorers. Long voyages became possible because of the development of ships like the caravel, which were sturdy enough to cross the Atlantic.

A Portuguese caravel

Around the world

Once a ship sails out of sight of land its captain needs a reliable method of navigation. The compass, the astrolabe (a device for measuring the height of the sun), and the globe were the basic tools, allowing navigators to plot a ship's voyage with some accuracy.

As long sea voyages became more common, more accurate tools for navigation were developed.

The legend of El Dorado

In the 16th century, a legend grew up concerning a South American king called "El Dorado", who had a horde of gold hidden in a city somewhere in the jungle. Over the centuries many have tried to find his "lost city", but neither it nor its fabulous treasure has ever been found.

Aztec gold figure

Gold coins

Spanish soldiers were paid in gold coins made from melted-down native artefacts. Spanish ships sailing from South American ports along the Caribbean coast provided rich pickings for pirates. Robinson Crusoe finds coins like these later in the story.

Spanish gold coins

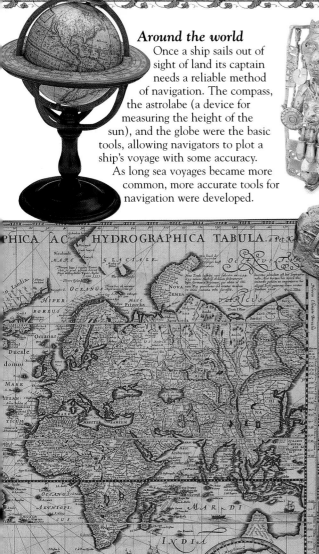

Mapping the world

Maps of the world changed greatly through the 16th and 17th centuries, with more and more of the Earth's lands and seas charted and named. By Defoe's time, this world map showed many landmasses quite accurately, but Europe is too large and the shape of North America is rather vague.

SLAVERY

In the 15th and 16th centuries, the trade in people was big business. When the sugar and tobacco plantations were started up in the New World, the settlers thought nothing of using slaves to work on the land.

Slave routes

Huge numbers of men, women, and children were transported from West Africa by ship to be put to work for European landowners.

Slave labour

In the Caribbean and Brazil, and later in the USA, slaves were made to work long hours on plantations or as servants in houses. They had no rights and were treated as property.

Spaniards on the island of Hispaniola, having exhausted the gold mines, force slaves to grow sugar.

This Brazilian view, by Jean J. Deltil, shows Europeans relaxing, while African slaves work the land.

Brazilian prosperity

In the story, Robinson Crusoe becomes involved in the profitable, but very cruel, slave trade, and makes a fortune easily from investing in a sugar plantation. In the 1600s Brazil was emerging as an economically strong country, and it was a good life for the owners of the slaves and the plantations.

Chapter one

MY FIRST VOYAGE

I WAS BORN IN THE YEAR 1632, in the city of York, of a good family. Being the third son and not bred to any trade, my heart was filled very early with rambling thoughts. My father designed me for the law, but I would be satisfied with nothing but going to sea.

My father, a wise and grave man, called me one morning into his chamber and told me it was for men of desperate fortunes on one hand, or of aspiring, superior fortune on the other, to go abroad upon adventures; that mine was the middle state, which he had found, by long experience, was the best state in the world and the most suited to human happiness.

He bid me observe that the middle station was not exposed to the miseries and hardships of the lower part of mankind, nor embarrassed with the pride, ambition, and envy of the upper part of mankind;

Execution of Charles I
Crusoe's "wise and grave" father is a member of the middle-class, which had grown rich and powerful at the time this story begins. The middle classes backed Parliament who fought King Charles I during the English Civil War (1642-51). The king lost, and was executed in 1649, when Robinson would have been 17.

A sensible career
Crusoe's father has high hopes that his son will follow a steady, respectable career, such as clerk to an attorney or lawyer (above). Guilt at not following his father's advice will prey heavily on Robinson's mind in the years to come.

My father designed me for the law, but I would be satisfied with nothing but going to sea.

that all agreeable diversions, and all desirable pleasures, were the blessings attending the middle station of life.

After this he pressed me in the most affectionate manner that he would endeavour to enter me fairly into the station of life which he had been just recommending to me. And he would venture to say to me that if I did take this foolish step, God would not bless me, and I would have leisure to reflect on having ignored his advice when there would be no one to help me.

Drunken sailors
For Robinson, like many young men of his time, the sea promised freedom and adventure. Sailors filled the inns of every seaport town, drinking and boasting about their adventures.

I was sincerely affected and resolved not to think of going abroad any more. But alas! A few days wore it all off and a few weeks after I resolved to run away. I told my mother that my thoughts were so entirely bent upon seeing the world that I should never settle to anything; that I was now 18 years old, which was too late to become an apprentice or a clerk to an attorney. This put my mother into a great passion and she wondered how I could think of any such thing after such kind and tender expressions as she knew my father had used to me. In short, if I would ruin myself there was no help for it, but I might depend I should never have their consent for it.

It was not till almost a year after this that I broke loose. I consulted neither father nor mother any more, but leaving them to hear of it as they might, without asking God's blessing or my father's, on the first of September 1651, I went on board a ship in the port of Hull bound for London.

Never did any young adventurer's misfortunes, I believe, begin sooner, or continue longer, than mine.

My thoughts were entirely bent upon seeing the world.

The sixth day of our being at sea we came in sight of Yarmouth. The wind being contrary, we were obliged to drop anchor. Our men spent the time in rest and mirth; but the eighth day, the wind increased.

The men roused me and told me that I was as able to pump as another.

By noon the sea was very high indeed. Now I began to see terror and amazement in the faces of the seamen. I was dreadfully frightened. I got out of my cabin, and looked out: the sea went mountains high, and broke upon us every three or four minutes.

In the middle of the night, one of the men cried out we had sprung a leak; another said there was four foot of water in the hold. Then all hands were called to the pump. My heart, as I thought, died within me and I fell backwards upon my bed. However, the men roused me, and told me that though I was able to do nothing before, I was as able to pump as another.

I stirred up and went to the pump, but, the water increasing in the hold, it soon became clear that the ship would founder.

Going south
Robinson heads for the nearest major port to his home town of York – Hull. From there he journeys by sea down the coast, until shipwrecked at Winterton, near Yarmouth.

A light ship launched a boat to help us, the men rowing very heartily and risking their lives to save ours. Our men cast them a rope and we hauled them close under our stern and got all into their boat. We were not much more than a quarter of an hour out of our ship when we saw her sink.

We were unable to reach the shore till past the lighthouse at Winterton. From there, we walked to Yarmouth, where we were treated with great humanity.

The master's son spoke to me after we were at Yarmouth two or three days, and told his father who I was, and how I had come on this voyage only for a trial.

"Young man," says the master, "perhaps this has all befallen us on your account, like Jonah in the Bible. I would not set my foot in the same ship as thee for a thousand pounds!" He told me to go back to my father, and not tempt Providence to my ruin.

We parted soon after, and I saw him no more. As to going home, it occurred to me how I should be laughed at among the neighbours, and should be ashamed to see, not my father and mother only, but even everybody else.

Uncertain what course to lead, I stayed awhile. And in time the memory of the distress I had been in wore off, and I looked out for a voyage.

Jonah is thrown into the sea.

A vast fish saves Jonah's life.

Jonah
In the Bible, Jonah disobeys God, who sends a storm to wreck the ship he is sailing in. The sailors realize Jonah has caused the storm and, to save their lives, throw him overboard. Ever since, anyone thought to bring bad luck is called a "Jonah".

Guiding lights
Lighthouses were placed all around the coast to warn sailors at night of rocks and sand banks or to mark a harbour entrance. The one at Winterton was built around 1616. Defoe stayed at Winterton in 1727.

The pump
This mechanical device in the bottom of a ship was used in storms to expel water that frequently seeped through the ship's timbers.

"I would not set my foot in the same ship as thee for a thousand pounds!"

11

Chapter two

THE PIRATES

THAT EVIL INFLUENCE which carried me away from my father's house next presented the most unfortunate of all enterprises to my view, and I went on board a vessel bound to the coast of Guinea. This was the only voyage which was successful in all my adventures, and which I owe to the integrity and honesty of the captain, under whom I also got a competent knowledge of the mathematics and the rules of navigation and learned how to keep an account of the ship's course, and to understand other things that were needful to be understood by a sailor. This voyage made me both a sailor and a merchant; for I brought home enough gold dust to bring me almost £300 in London.

This was the only voyage which was successful in all my adventures.

I was now set up as a Guinea trader, and I resolved to make the same voyage again. Our ship, making her course towards the Canary Islands, was surprised in the grey of the morning by a Turkish rover from Sallee, who gave chase with all the sail she could make. We also crowded as much canvas as our yards would spread; but finding the pirate gaining upon us, we prepared to fight, our ship having 12 guns and the rogue 18.

The pirate attack
The pirates attack on one quarter (the ship's side, near the stern); the sailors move eight cannons there to repel them. The pirates then attack on the other quarter, before the sailors can move the cannons across the deck.

Ship's cannon
Cannons fired stone or iron balls weighing several kilos. These did not explode, but caused considerable damage.

About three in the afternoon he caught up with us, and bringing to by mistake just athwart our quarter, instead of our stern, we brought eight guns to bear on that side, and poured in a broadside, which made him sheer off again. He prepared to attack us again, and we to defend ourselves; but laying us on board the next time upon our other quarter, he entered sixty men upon our decks, who fell to cutting and hacking the decks and rigging.

We cleared our deck of them twice, however, our ship being disabled, and three of our men killed, and eight wounded, we were obliged to yield.

The pirate ship entered sixty men upon our decks.

Pirate port
The port of Sallee (now called Salé) on the Moroccan coast was once a notorious pirate haunt. It lies across the Bouregreg River from the capital of Morocco, Rabat.

I was made a slave, being young and nimble.

We were all carried as prisoners into Sallee, a port belonging to the Moors. I was kept by the captain of the rover, and made his slave, being young and nimble. I meditated nothing but my escape, but found no way that had the least probability in it.

After about two years, an odd circumstance presented itself. My patron, lying at home longer than usual, used to take the ship's pinnace and go out into the open sea a-fishing. As I was a skilled fisherman, he never went without me.

It happened that he had arranged to go out in this boat with two or three Moors of some distinction. He had therefore sent on board a larger store of provisions than usual, and had ordered me to get ready three guns with powder and shot, for they designed some sport of fowling as well as fishing.

By and by my patron told me his guests had put off going and ordered me and a Moor to go out and catch some fish, for his friends were to sup at his house.

After we had fished some time and caught nothing, for when I had a fish on my hook, I would not pull it up, I said to the Moor, "Our master will not be thus served, we must go farther off."

He, thinking no harm, agreed and set the sails; I ran the boat further out to sea, and, making as if I stooped for something behind him, I tossed him clear overboard into the sea. Fetching one of the guns, I told him I had done him no hurt, "but if you come near the boat I'll shoot you through the head, for I am resolved to have my liberty."

So he swam for the shore, and I make no doubt he reached it with ease, for he was an excellent swimmer.

I tossed him clear overboard into the sea.

Such was the fright I had of falling into the Moors' hands, that I sailed five days without once going on shore.

When I knew I was out of their reach, I saw a Portuguese ship, which, it seems, saw me and shortened sail to let me come up. They invited me to come on board and very kindly took me in. It was an inexpressible joy to me, that anyone will believe. We had a very good voyage to the Brazils, and arrived in the Bay de Todos los Santos, or All-Saints' Bay, in about 22 days.

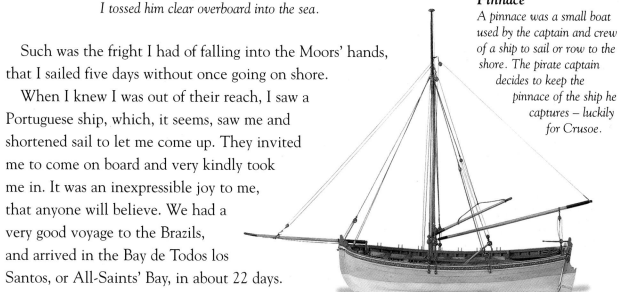

Pinnace
A pinnace was a small boat used by the captain and crew of a ship to sail or row to the shore. The pirate captain decides to keep the pinnace of the ship he captures – luckily for Crusoe.

A SAILOR'S LIFE

FOR A RECKLESS YOUNG MAN like Robinson Crusoe, life at sea promised adventure, fame and fortune, but it also meant enduring hardship and danger. Living conditions for the crew on board a 17th-century merchant ship were extremely tough and the food – and the pay – were poor. Discipline on board was so harsh that the sailors sometimes mutinied, taking command of the ship and becoming pirates. Besides these hazards, there was also the risk of storms, shipwreck, sickness – and attack by ruthless pirates.

The Shipwreck by Ivan C. Aivazoffski, 1873.

Rowing for their lives
Their ship having run on the rocks in a storm, the crew escapes in the longboat – a common enough scene of distress from the days of wooden sailing ships.

LIFE ON SHIP

Voyages lasted many months in cramped, dirty conditions. Fruit and vegetables soon ran out, and sailors suffered from a poor diet. This often led to scurvy – a disease caused by lack of vitamin C.

Hard tack biscuit
Sailors mostly lived on bread, salted meat, and rock-hard biscuits called hard tack. They also caught fish fresh from the sea.

Sweet dreams
Sailors often slept in a canvas hammock. This was adapted from a hanging bed Christopher Columbus had first seen being used by West Indian natives in the 1490s. A hammock wrapped around the sleeper and swung with the motion of the ship, ensuring a more restful night.

Rats in the hold
Rats were a serious nuisance on a ship, stealing food, gnawing ropes, and spreading disease. They made their homes in the darkness of a ship's hold, where the cargo was stored.

Mizzen mast

Poop deck

Stern (back of ship)

Shroud

Main mast

Quarterdeck

Merchant ship
Dating from the early 17th century, this Dutch-designed merchant ship is probably similar to those sailed in by Robinson Crusoe.

Rudder

Sternpost

Keel

Rough weather
Ships were quite small and not very stable. In rough weather they could lurch and roll alarmingly. Anyone turning in for the night could quickly find themselves turned out!

Seasick
Perhaps the most unpleasant effects of a storm at sea was seasickness – something that Robinson Crusoe himself suffers from on his first voyage.

Yard (wooden spar from which sail hangs)

Fore topmast

Fore mast

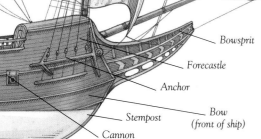

Bowsprit

Forecastle

Anchor

Stempost

Cannon

Bow (front of ship)

ALEXANDER SELKIRK

Alexander Selkirk (1676–1721) is the likely model for Robinson Crusoe. The son of a Scottish shoemaker, Selkirk ran away to sea and joined a pirate ship. After falling out with the captain, he was put ashore on the desert island of Juan Fernandez in September 1704.

The Pacific island of Juan Fernandez.

Island life
Selkirk only had basic supplies, including a gun and ammunition, a knife, an axe, a kettle, and a Bible. He lived off wild goats, tamed cats, and read the Bible.

Juan Fernandez – as drawn by Selkirk.

Rescued!
Selkirk was rescued in February 1709 by an English ship commanded by Woodes Rogers. Rogers gave details of the event in a book entitled *Voyage Round the World*. The book was widely read and Defoe certainly knew of it.

The Bounty
Sailors sometimes rebelled against the discipline imposed upon them and mutinied. One of the best-known instances occurred on *HMS Bounty* in 1789, when mutineers led by Fletcher Christian, the master's mate, cast the captain, William Bligh, and 18 others adrift in an open boat.

Anthony Hopkins as Captain Bligh and Mel Gibson as mutineer Fletcher Christian in The Bounty (1984).

TERRORS OF THE SEAS
Pirates preyed on the cargoes of merchantmen. The Barbary corsairs (pirates) of the southern Mediterranean, whom Robinson Crusoe encounters, were among the most feared. Unlike most pirates, they sold their prisoners as slaves.

The Jolly Roger – a notorious pirate emblem.

Close combat
A pirate captain's usual plan of attack was to steer right up to the side of a merchant ship. Then hordes of pirates, armed to the teeth, would swarm aboard, overpower the crew, and capture the cargo.

Barbary galley
Packed with fighting men, a Barbary corsair's galley was powered by oars pulled by slaves, as well as by sails. It was swift enough to catch most large craft.

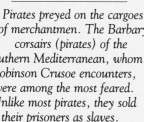

Pirate treasure
Trinkets and jewels, stripped from wealthy passengers, made a haul all pirates relished. The booty taken in a raid was carefully divided up according to a pirate's rank, with the captain getting the lion's share.

Chapter three

Shipwrecked!

THE GENEROUS CAPTAIN would take nothing for my passage. I made about 220 pieces of eight from all my cargo, and with this stock I went on shore. Seeing how well the planters lived and how they quickly grew rich, I acquainted myself with the manner of their planting and making of sugar, and resolved to settle there.

But alas! I had fallen into an employment directly contrary to the life I delighted in.

Having lived almost four years in the Brazils, and beginning to thrive and prosper, I had made friends of some of the merchants at St Salvador, our port. I had frequently given them an account of my two voyages to the coast of Guinea, and it happened that three of them told me they had a mind to fit out a ship to go there. The question was, whether I would manage the trading part upon the coast of Guinea.

I that was born to be my own destroyer told them that I would go with all my heart if they would look after my plantation. The same day I went on board we set sail for the African coast.

We had very good weather all the way upon our own coast and were by our last observation in 7 degrees 22 minutes northern latitude, when a violent tornado took us quite out of our knowledge. It blew in such terrible manner we could do nothing but let it carry us wherever fate and the fury of the winds directed. About the twelfth day, the weather abating a little, the master began to consult with me what course he should take, for the ship was leaky

The merchants had a mind to fit out a ship to go to Guinea.

Spanish silver
A piece of eight was a silver Spanish coin. It was a common currency in the Caribbean region. Crusoe's haul of 220 pieces of eight would have been worth about £3,500 today.

"Our English islands"
In the 17th century, Britain, Spain, and France vied for the islands of the Caribbean. Several had become British colonies, such as Barbados (in 1626), Jamaica (seized from Spain in 1655), and Antigua (in 1667).

and very much disabled. We changed our course and steered NW by W in order to reach some of our English islands in the Caribbean, such as Barbados. But our voyage was otherwise determined, for a second storm came upon us.

In this distress, the wind blowing very hard, one of our men early in the morning cried out, "Land!" No sooner had we run out of the cabin than the ship struck upon a sandbank, and, in a moment, her motion being so stopped, the sea broke over her.

A violent tornado took us quite out of our knowledge.

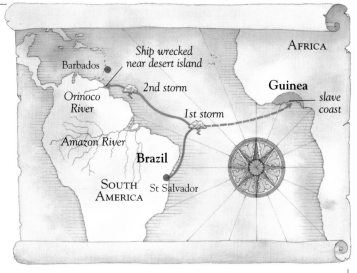

----> Planned route ——→ Actual route

A doomed voyage
Robinson Crusoe plans to sail from St Salvador in Brazil to the coast of Guinea in West Africa to pick up slaves. Two storms blow the ship completely off course.

*A raging wave
overturned the boat.*

Clinging to the rock
*Robinson Crusoe survives
the raging sea by clinging to
a rock, which, in Christian
tradition, symbolizes faith.
The author, Daniel Defoe,
hints that only faith in God
will save Crusoe from the
perils and trials he is to face.*

We sat looking at one another,
expecting death, for we imagined the ship would break
into pieces. We had a boat at our stern and slung her over the ship's
side; getting into her we committed ourselves, being eleven in
number, to God's mercy and the wild sea.

After we had rowed about a league and a
half towards land, a raging wave, mountain-like,
took us with such fury that it overturned the boat.
We were all swallowed up in a moment.

Though I swam very well I could not draw breath till the wave,
having driven me towards the shore, went back and left me half
dead. I got upon my feet and endeavoured to make towards the land,
but the sea came after me. A wave buried me twenty or thirty feet
deep and I could feel myself carried with a mighty force towards the
shore. Twice more I was lifted up by the waves and carried forwards.
The last time was nearly fatal to me, for the sea dashed me against a
rock with such force that it beat the breath from my body. I
recovered a little and resolved to hold fast till the wave went back.
Then I ran towards the mainland, clambered up the shore, and sat
down upon the grass, free from danger.

I thanked God that my life was saved, reflecting upon all my comrades, and that there should not be one soul saved but myself. Yet I was wet, had no clothes, nor anything to eat or drink. I had no weapons either to hunt and kill any creature for my sustenance, or to defend myself. I walked about a furlong from the shore, to see if I could find water to drink, which I did, to my great joy.

Night coming upon me, all I could think of was to get up into a thick bushy tree and sit all night, and consider what death I should die, for as yet I saw no prospect of life.

Desert island
In Crusoe's time, few sailors were able to swim, which could explain why he is the only one to survive. Crusoe is washed up on a desert island in the Caribbean.

I could feel myself carried with a mighty force towards the shore.

Chapter four

THE WRECK

Slippery slope
It is no wonder that Crusoe had difficulty getting on board, for the sides of the ship would have been high and the hull's wet timbers extremely slippery. He finally manges to clamber up into the ship's forecastle. This was situated in the bows and was where the crew lived and where equipment was stored.

WHEN I WAKED IT WAS BROAD DAY, the weather clear, and the storm abated. The ship was lifted off from the sand, and driven up almost as far as the rock where I had been so bruised. The ship seeming to stand upright still, I wished myself on board that I might save some necessary things for my use.

A little after noon the tide ebbed so far out that I could walk within a quarter of a mile of the ship. I saw that if we had kept on board, we had been all safe, and I had not been so miserable as to be left destitute of all company. This forced tears from my eyes, but as there was little relief in that, I resolved, if possible, to get to the ship. I pulled off my clothes, for the weather was hot to extremity, and took to the water.

When I came to the ship I did not know how to get on board. As she lay high out of the water, there was nothing within my reach to lay hold of. I swam around her twice, and the second time I spied a rope, which I wondered I did not see at first. With great difficulty I got hold of it and climbed up into the forecastle of the ship.

Seaman's chest
Space on board ship was very limited, so a sailor used to keep all his personal belongings – clothes, tools, weapons, and trinkets – in a wooden sea chest. When closed, the chest served as a table or a seat.

My first work was to see what was spoiled and what was free. I found that all the provisions were dry and I filled my pockets with biscuit, and ate it as I went about other things.

There were several spare beams and a spare top-mast or two, I flung them overboard and then went down the ship's side. I tied them together to form a raft and found I could walk upon it very well, and that it was strong enough to bear any reasonable weight.

I first got three of the seamen's chests; the first I filled with provisions and I found clothes enough for present use. After long searching I found the carpenter's chest, which was indeed much more valuable than a shipload of gold. There were two fowling-pieces in the great cabin, and two pistols, and a small bag of shot, and two old rusty swords. I found three barrels of gunpowder, two of them dry, the third had taken water. We had in the ship a dog and two cats. I carried both the cats with me, and as for the dog, he jumped out of the ship and swam on shore with me.

Having loaded my raft, I put to sea back to the island. A little distant from the place where I had landed before there appeared some creek or river there, so I guided my raft as well as I could to keep to the middle stream. I spied a little cove on the right and thrust my raft upon that flat piece of ground.

Swiss Family Robinson
A family is shipwrecked on a desert island and salvages the wreck for equipment just like Robinson Crusoe, in Johann Wyss's classic adventure story The Swiss Family Robinson. *It was first published in 1812.*

My next work was to view the country, and seek a proper place for my habitation. There was a hill not above a mile from me, which rose up very steep and high. After I had with great difficulty got to the top, I saw that I was on an island surrounded on all sides by sea. It was barren, and, as I saw good reason to believe, uninhabited.

I came back to my raft, and fell to work to bring my cargo on shore. I barricaded myself around with the chests and boards and made a kind of hut for that night's lodging.

I resolved to make another voyage out to the ship and to set all other things aside till I had got everything out. I brought away bags of nails and spikes; hatchets; some rope; two barrels of musket bullets; seven muskets, gunpowder, and a large bag full of small shot. Besides these things I took a sail, a hammock, and some bedding. I got several things of less value, but not at all less useful to me; such as pens, ink, paper, three or four compasses, and books of navigation and three Bibles.

Having got my second cargo on shore, I went to work to make myself a little tent. When I had done this, spreading one of the beds upon the ground, laying my two pistols just at my head, I went to bed for the first time.

Over the following thirteen days, I went on board the ship eleven times and brought away all that one pair of hands could well be supposed capable of bringing.

The twelfth time I found some European coins, and some pieces of eight, some gold, some silver. I smiled to myself at the sight of this money. "Oh drug!" said I aloud. "What are you good for? I have no manner of use for you; I shall leave you here."

However, upon second thoughts, I took the money away.

It blew very hard all that night, and in the morning when I looked out, behold, no more ship was to be seen.

Barrels

Precious cargo
*Good fortune – or God –
certainly smiles on Robinson
Crusoe, allowing him to
salvage all kinds of useful
things from the wreck.*

Bullets for
a musket
(type of gun).

Gunpowder

Compass

Rope

Spike for
separating
rope strands.

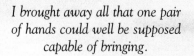

*I brought away all that one pair
of hands could well be supposed
capable of bringing.*

Worthless money
*Crusoe calls money a
"drug" because people are
"addicted" to getting as much
as they can; yet, if money
cannot be used in trade, it
has no value at all.*

Chapter five

ON A DESERT ISLE

Before I set up my tent, I pitched two rows of strong stakes. This fence was so strong that neither man nor beast could get over it.

I HAD MANY THOUGHTS of what kind of dwelling to make, whether I should make a cave in the earth, or a tent; and, in short, I resolved upon both. I consulted several things; firstly, health and fresh water; secondly, a shelter from sun; thirdly, security from ravenous creatures, whether men or beasts; fourthly, a view of the sea, so I might not miss any chance of being rescued.

I found a little plain on the side of a hill. On the side of the rock there was a hollow, like the entrance of a cave. On the flat green just before the hollow I pitched my tent.

Before I set up my tent I pitched two rows of strong stakes. This fence was so strong that neither man nor beast could get over it. The entrance I made to be not by a door, but by a short ladder to go over the top. When I was inside, I lifted the ladder over after me. Into this fortress I carried all my provisions, ammunition, and stores.

I then began to work my way into the rock, and thus I made a cave just behind my tent, which served me like a cellar. It cost me much labour and many days before all these things were brought to perfection.

I went out with my gun at least once every day. I presently discovered that there were goats on the island, which was a great satisfaction to me.

After I had been there about ten or twelve days, it came into my thoughts that I should lose my reckoning of time. To prevent this, I made a great cross and set it up on the shore where I first landed. I cut with a knife in large capitals:

"I CAME ON SHORE HERE ON THE 3OTH OF SEPT. 1659."

Upon the sides of this post I cut every day a notch with my knife, and thus I kept my calendar, or weekly, monthly and yearly reckoning of time.

I now began to consider seriously my condition, and drew up my state of affairs in writing; the comforts I enjoyed against the miseries I suffered.

To prevent losing my reckoning of time, I made a great cross and set it up on the shore.

Silver linings
Crusoe's list of the good points and the bad points about his situation reveals to him that he has much to be thankful for.

EVIL

I am cast upon a horrible desolate island.

I am divided from mankind, banished from human society.

I have not clothes to cover me.

I am without any defence or means to resist any violence of man or beast.

I have no soul to speak to, or to comfort me.

GOOD

But I am alive, and not drowned as all my ship's company was.

But I am not starved and perishing in a barren place.

But I am in a hot climate where if I had clothes I would hardly wear them.

But I am cast on an island where I see no wild beasts to hurt me.

But God wonderfully sent the ship in near enough to the shore, that I have gotten out many things to supply my wants, as long as I live.

I was perfectly astonished when I saw about ten or twelve ears of green barley.

Barley
Barley was probably one of the first crops to be cultivated – in Egypt c.5000 BC. It is a tough plant, grows quickly and needs little rain, so it is quite possible it could have sprung up by accident, as Crusoe describes.

It happened that, rummaging through my things, I found a little bag. I saw nothing in it but husks and dust, and wishing to have the bag for some other use, I shook the husks out of it on one side of my fortification under the rock.

I was perfectly astonished when, sometime later, I saw about ten or twelve ears of green barley. I began to think that God had miraculously caused this grain to grow, without any help of seed, purely for my sustenance.

At last I remembered that I had shaken a bag of chicken's food out in that place, and then the wonder began to cease. I must confess, my religious thankfulness to God's providence began to abate, too.

I carefully saved the ears of corn and resolved to sow them all again, hoping in time to grow enough corn to supply me with bread.

I worked excessive hard these three or four months to get my walls done; and on the 14th April I closed it up so that nothing could come at me, unless it could first mount my wall.

Having settled my household stuff and habitation, I began to keep a journal. I shall here give you a copy as long as it lasted, for having no more ink I was forced to leave it off.

April 17th: as I was busy in the entrance to my cave, I was terribly frightened by a most dreadful, surprising thing. The earth suddenly came crumbling down from the roof and from the edge of the hill over my head, and two of the posts I had set up in the cave cracked in a frightful manner. I was heartily scared, thinking my cave was falling in.

I ran to my ladder and got over my wall fearing that pieces of the hill might roll down on me.

I plainly saw it was a terrible earthquake.

I plainly saw it was a terrible earthquake; the motion of the earth made my stomach sick like one tossed at sea. After the third shock was over, and I felt no more for some time, I began to take courage; yet I had not heart enough to go over my wall again, for fear of being buried alive. All this while I had not the least religious thought, nothing but the common "Lord have mercy upon me."

   The wind soon rose and, in less than half an hour, it blew a most dreadful hurricane. The sea was covered over with foam and froth, the waves covered the shore, the trees were torn up by the roots. The storm lasted about three hours, and in two hours more it began to rain very hard. All this while I sat upon the ground very much terrified and dejected, not knowing what to do.

Wind and rain
Hurricanes occur in the Caribbean, though usually in autumn not in April, as in Crusoe's account. Winds of over 160 km/h (100 mph) lash coasts, whipping up huge waves. The winds bring torrential rain.

For some weeks I considered moving my tent from under the hanging precipice of the hill. However it occurred to me that it would require a vast amount of time to do this.

June 18th: rained all day. The rain felt cold, and I was something chilly, which I knew was not usual.

June 20th: no rest all night, violent pains in my head, and feverish.

June 21st: very ill, frightened almost to death with the fears of my sad condition.

June 27th: the ague again so violent that I lay a-bed all day. I had not stomach to stand up, or to get myself any water to drink. I prayed to God, "Lord pity me. Lord have mercy upon me." I fell asleep and had this terrible dream.

I thought that I was sitting outside my wall and that I saw a man descend from a black cloud. He was all over as bright as flame; his countenance was most inexpressibly dreadful. He was no sooner landed upon the earth, but he moved towards me. He spoke to me in a voice most terrible: "Seeing all these things have not brought thee to repentance, now thou shalt die." He lifted up the spear that was in his hand, to kill me. I awoke and found it was but a dream.

I began to reproach myself for my past life. The good advice of my father came to mind, that if I went to sea, God would not bless me, and that I would have leisure hereafter to reflect upon having neglected his counsel.

June 28th: I got up but was very weak. That night before I lay down, I did what I had never done before: I kneeled down and prayed to God that if I called upon Him in the day of trouble, He would deliver me. After my broken and imperfect prayer was over I fell into a sound sleep.

When I awaked I found myself exceedingly refreshed; I gave God thanks for my recovery from my sickness. I read the Bible, and promised myself to read some pages every morning and every night.

His countenance was most inexpressibly dreadful.

An angel weighs souls on the Day of Judgement.

Demon vision
In his dream, Crusoe is terrified by a demon from his own guilty conscience. His father and God have become muddled in his mind. By rejecting one, he believes he has rejected the other and deserves death.

The country
appeared so fresh, so
green, so flourishing
that it looked like a
planted garden.

I had now been on this unhappy island above ten months, and all possibility of deliverance seemed to be entirely taken from me. It was the 15th July when I began to make a more detailed survey of the island.

I went up the creek where I had brought my raft on shore. After I came about two miles up I found many pleasant meadows and divers plants which I had no notion of.

The next day I went up the same way, and after going some way farther, the country became more woody. Here there were different fruits, particularly melons and grapes. I spent all that evening there, which was the first night I had lain from home.

The following morning I travelled the length of the valley. The country appeared so fresh, so green, so flourishing that it looked like a planted garden. I saw here an abundance of cocoa, orange, and lemon and citron trees. I resolved to lay up a store to furnish myself for the wet season.

When I came home from this journey, I contemplated that most pleasant fruitful part of the island and that I had pitched my home in by far the worst part of the country. I resolved not to remove my home, but I spent much of my time in this delicious vale. I built me a little bower and surrounded it with a strong fence; and here I lay very secure, sometimes two or three nights; so that I fancied now I had my country house, and my sea-coast house.

September 30th: I had now come to the unhappy anniversary of my landing on the island. I counted up the notches on my post, and found that I had been on shore three hundred and sixty five days. I kept this day as a solemn fast, setting it apart to religious exercise. At last, having not tasted any food for twelve hours, I ate a biscuit cake and a bunch of grapes, and went to bed, finishing the day as I began it.

Paradise garden
The valley recalls the Garden of Eden in the Bible, where God allowed Adam, the first man, to live. Crusoe later thinks of the valley as an example of God's bounty.

Orange

Cocoa

Lemon

Fruits of the forest
Crusoe's description accurately reflects the abundance of fruits that grow in the fertile, tropical islands of the Caribbean.

Tropical forest
Crusoe finds lush forest similar to that of Trinidad, which author Daniel Defoe may have used as a model for his fictional island.

Fashionably dressed

While Crusoe was roaming his island dressed in skins, fashions for men in England had reached unprecedented heights of extravagance. This debonair man-about-town would have found Crusoe's home-made get-up hilarious.

By now my clothes began to decay, mightily. It was a great help that I had some three dozen shirts which I found in the chests of the seamen. There were also several thick coats but they were too hot to wear, and I had worn out all the waistcoats. Though it is true that the weather was so violent hot that there was no need of clothes, yet I could not go quite naked; nay, the very heat frequently blistered my skin or gave me the headache.

I had saved the skins of all the creatures that I killed. So I set to work a tailoring, or rather, indeed, a-botching; for if I was a bad carpenter, I was a worse tailor. The first thing I made was a cap for my head, with the hair on the outside to shoot off the rain. After this I made a waistcoat and breeches open at the knees. I then spent a great deal of time and pains to make me an umbrella. I covered it with skins, the hair upward, so that it cast off the rains and kept the sun off so effectually that I could walk out in the hottest weather; and when I had no need of it, could close and carry it under my arm.

If anyone in England had seen me in such dress it must either have frightened them, or raised a great deal of laughter. I had a great high shapeless cap, made of goat's skin with a flap hanging down behind as well to keep the sun from me as to shoot the rain off from running down my neck. I had a jacket of goatskin, the skirts coming down to about the middle of my thighs and a pair of open-kneed breeches of the same.

I had a broad goatskin belt, and there hung a little saw and a hatchet. I had another belt over my shoulder with two pouches, for my powder and shot.

At back I carried my basket, in my hand my gun, and over my head my great, clumsy, goatskin umbrella.

Crusoe's gun

Robinson Crusoe found several guns on board the wreck, which he used to shoot animals and birds for food and skins. By 1659, the year of Crusoe's shipwreck, hunting with guns was an established pastime. This detail of a man hunting birds from the late 16th-century Bradford Table Carpet is one of the earliest depictions of the sport.

At back I carried my basket, in my hand my gun, and over my head my great, clumsy, goatskin umbrella. My beard I had once suffered to grow till it was about a quarter of a yard long, but as I had both scissors and razor, I had cut it pretty short, except what grew on my upper lip. This I had trimmed into a pair of whiskers, monstrous in length and shape, such as in England would have passed for frightful.

Chapter six

ISLAND LIFE

I CANNOT SAY THAT in the following years any extraordinary thing happened to me. In general it may be observed that I was very seldom idle.

"In the dry season, my yearly labour was to harvest my barley and prepare land sufficient for the next crop. This I sowed just before the wet season – the same quantity each year – in hopes that it would fully supply me with bread."

"During the wet months I sat within doors. I diverted myself with talking to the young parrot I had caught. I quickly taught him to know his name "Poll"; but it was some years before he could call me by my name."

"After an absence, one of my cats came home with three kittens. From these three, I afterwards came to be so pestered with cats I had to drive them from my house."

"All I could make use of was all that was valuable to me. I had a parcel of money but, alas!, there the nasty, sorry, useless stuff lay. I would have given it all away for a sixpennyworth of turnip or carrot seed from England, or a bottle of ink."

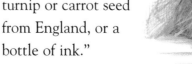

"For want of tools, want of help, and want of skill, everything was a vast labour and required prodigious time to do. I was full two and forty days making me a board for a long shelf; whereas two sawyers would have cut six in half a day."

"My dog surprised a young kid and I caught it and saved it alive. The creature became so loving, so gentle, and so fond, that it became one of my domestics, and would never leave me afterwards."

"I discovered, after many misshapen failures, how to make pots and plates out of clay."

"I employed myself in making a great many baskets, though I didn't finish them very handsomely."

"My daily labour was going out with my gun for food. I also had a great mind to see the whole island and travelled across to the west. Here I found it much pleasanter; the shore was covered with innumerable turtles and wild fowls; and many of them very good meat."

Thus I lived mighty comfortably, but in the same course, in the same posture and place, for five years.

Mallet

Adze

A dugout canoe, with tools for hollowing it out.

Chapter seven

A PERILOUS VOYAGE

IN MY TRAVELS ACROSS THE ISLAND, I came within view of the sea to the west. There, at a very great distance, I saw land, and I resolved to make a vessel from the trunk of a tree.

It took me twenty days to fell the tree; fourteen days getting the branches off; and one month to shape it. It cost me three months to hollow the inside till it was a handsome boat, big enough for twenty-six men. But it was one hundred yards from the water, and all my attempts to launch it failed. I was obliged to let it lie where it was, as a reminder to teach me to be wiser next time.

I never gave up hopes of having a boat, though I was near two years about it. I finished a little canoe; but its smallness put an end to venturing over the sea to that land to the west.

Now I merely thought of sailing around the island. For this purpose I fitted a little mast to my boat and made a sail out of some of the pieces of the ship's sails, of which I had a great stock. I made little lockers at either end of my boat to hold provisions and fixed my umbrella at the stern to keep the heat of the sun off me.

It was the 6th of November, in my sixth year of captivity, that I set out. On the east side of the island I came to a great ledge of rock and sandbank stretching into the sea; I was obliged to go a great way out to navigate around it, and found myself in a current like the sluice of a mill. There was no wind stirring to help me and it carried my boat with such violence farther into the vast ocean that I began to give myself up for lost. I had no prospect before me but of starving for hunger. And now I saw how easy it was for the providence of God to make the most miserable condition mankind could be in, *worse*. Now I looked back upon my desolate, solitary island as the most pleasant place in the world.

Then about noon, I felt a little breeze on my face and in half an hour it blew a pretty small, gentle gale. How gladly I spread my sail, running cheerfully before the wind and steering directly for land.

About four in the afternoon I reached my beloved island. There I fell upon my knees and gave God thanks for my deliverance.

I stowed my boat securely on this northern shore, and contented myself that I had had enough of rambling to sea for some time.

Wayana Indians from French Guiana use fire to dry out a freshly cut canoe.

Basic boat
A dugout canoe is one of the simplest types of boats to make. They were first made by primitive people more than 8,000 years ago. These logboats ride low in the water and so are not suitable for choppy seas.

Now I looked back upon my desolate, solitary island as the most pleasant place in the world.

A parrot called Poll

In this chapter, Robinson Crusoe pretends he is a king dining in his banqueting hall.
He jokes that Poll the parrot is the only one of his "servants" allowed to talk to him. Of course, Poll, thanks to Crusoe's teaching, is the only one able to talk!

The stoics

Founded by the philosopher Zeno, the stoics of ancient Greece were a group of thinkers who claimed to be above feeling pleasure or pain. Crusoe imagines that even these miserable souls would have had to smile at the sight of him and his animal "family".

Real-life Crusoe

Daniel Defoe partly based Robinson Crusoe on the true story of Scottish sailor Alexander Selkirk, who was marooned in 1704. Like Crusoe, Selkirk found goats and cats on his desert island. To while away the time, he taught them to dance, as this 18th-century print shows.

Chapter eight

A FAMILY DINNER

IN THE FIFTEENTH YEAR of my residence, my supply of gunpowder had begun to run low. If I expected to supply myself with goat flesh, breeding some tame was my only way. So I tried to think of some way to trap and snare goats.

I dug several large pits where I had observed the goats used to feed. At length, going there one morning, I found in one three kids, a male and two females.

I resolved to build an enclosure for them adjoining my country house. With infinite labour I fenced a proper piece of ground where there was likely to be herbage for them to eat, water, and cover to keep them from the sun. In about a year and a half I had a flock of about twelve goats, kids and all; and in two years more I had three and forty. I considered they would be a living store of flesh, milk, butter, and cheese for me as long as I lived in the place.

How mercifully can our great Creator treat his creatures, even in those conditions in which they seem to be overwhelmed by destruction! What a table was here spread for me in the wilderness, where I saw nothing at first but to perish for hunger!

It would have made a stoic smile to have seen me and my little family sit down to dinner; there was my majesty the prince and lord of the whole island. How like a king I dined, too, all alone, attended by my servants. Poll was the only person permitted to talk to me. My dog, who was now grown very old and frail, always sat at my right hand; and two cats, one on one side of the table, and one on the other, expecting now and then a bit from my hand.

With this attendance and in this plentiful manner I lived; neither could I be said to want anything but society, and of that, in some time after this, I was like to have too much.

Me and my little family sit down to dinner.

Chapter nine

THE FOOTPRINT

IT HAPPENED ONE DAY ABOUT NOON, going towards my boat, I was exceedingly surprised by the print of a man's naked foot on the shore. I stood like one thunderstruck, or as if I had seen an apparition: I listened, I looked round me; I went up the shore and down the shore but I could see no other impression but that one.

I was exceedingly surprised by the print of a man's naked foot on the shore.

I fled home, like one pursued; terrified, looking behind me at every two or three steps, mistaking every bush and tree, and fancying every stump to be a man.

The farther I was from the occasion of my fright, the greater my apprehensions were. Sometimes I fancied it must be the Devil in human shape. It came also into my thoughts that this foot might be the print of my own foot. Heartening myself therefore I began to peep abroad again, but could not persuade myself fully of this till I should go measure the mark. I found my foot not so large by a great deal. This discovery gave me the vapours again to the highest degree. I was sure that some man or men had been on the shore; or, that the island was inhabited.

I presently concluded that it must be some of the savages of the mainland that were gone away again to sea, being as loth, perhaps to have stayed in this desolate island as I would have been to have had them.

Oh what ridiculous resolutions men take when possessed with fear! The first thing I proposed to myself was to throw down my enclosures and turn all my animals into the woods; dig up my fields; then demolish my country house that they might not see any vestiges of habitation.

I waked much better composed, and resolved to build an outer wall thickened with timber, old cables, and everything I could think of; having in it seven holes to plant my seven muskets. In the inside of this, I raised my wall to above ten foot with earth. When this was done I stuck all the ground without my wall with stakes or sticks of the osier-like wood, which I found so apt to grow.

In two years' time I had a thick grove, and in five or six years a wood before my dwelling growing so monstrously thick and strong that it was perfectly impassable. No men would ever imagine that there was anything beyond it, much less a habitation. Thus I took all the measures prudence could suggest for my own preservation.

The Devil perches on a victim, an illustration by Frank Pape from *The Book of Psalms* (1914).

Mark of the Devil?
Alone and lonely on his island, Crusoe at first believes that the Devil has arrived just to upset his peace of mind. Later he mocks himself for being so foolish.

"Osier-like" sticks
Osiers are thin, flexible willow branches usually used for making baskets. The sticks Crusoe finds grow when stuck in the ground, creating, in time, a hedge to conceal his home.

Human sacrifice
It is likely that the natives (whom Crusoe calls "savages") brought their prisoners to this isolated spot, killed, and ate them, not out of hunger, but as part of a religious rite.

My search for secure places to hide my goats took me to the farthest south-west tip of the island. There I discovered a hill and made my way down to the shoreline.

It is not possible to express the horror of my mind at seeing the shore spread with skulls, hands, feet, and other bones of human bodies. There had been a fire within a circle dug out of the earth, where savages had sat down to their inhuman feastings upon the bodies of their fellow creatures.

I turned away from the horrid spectacle, ran up the hill as quickly as I could, and went home to my castle. There I gave God thanks that I was cast upon this side of the island where the savages never came. I had been here about

The shore was spread with skulls, hands, feet, and other bones of human bodies.

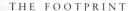

eighteen years, and now for about two years after this I kept close to my castle, my country house, and my enclosure. I never fired my gun once, though I never went out without it. I carried also three pistols in my belt and a great cutlass hanging at my side. I was now a most formidable fellow to look at. Every morning I made my tour to the hill to keep watch for any boats.

Every morning I made my tour to the hill to keep watch for any boats.

During this time I brooded on how I might destroy some of these monsters, or at least frighten them so as to prevent their coming hither any more.

I proposed that I would place myself in ambush where I might observe them; then, with my three guns, and in the middle of their bloody ceremony, let fly at them, and then fall upon them with my sword.

Later I began with cooler and calmer thoughts to consider what authority I had to be judge and executioner upon these men, whom heaven had thought fit to suffer unpunished. It is certain these people think it no more a crime to kill a captive taken in war than we do to kill an ox, nor to eat human flesh than we do to eat mutton.

I began, little by little, to be off my plan to attack these savages; that it was not my business to meddle with them, unless they first attacked me: and if they should, then I knew my duty.

Cannibals
To Europeans of Crusoe's time, cannibalism was the ultimate crime against humanity. Native peoples that practised, or were believed to practise it, were treated with terrible cruelty.

I was now in my twenty-third year of residence on this island. I had taught my Poll to speak and he talked so articulately and plain that it was very pleasant to me. My dog was a loving companion to me for most of my time, and then died of mere old age. And as for my cats, they multiplied and ran wild into the woods, except two or three favourites which I kept tame.

I always kept two or three kids, which I taught to feed out of my hand; and I had two more parrots which talked pretty well. I had also several tame seabirds, who I caught upon the shore; and the little stakes which I had planted before my castle wall now being grown up to a good thick grove, these birds lived among these low trees, which was very agreeable to me.

I would have been very well contented, if I could have lived safe from the dread of the savages. Now I dared not to drive a nail or chop a stick for fear the noise should be heard, much less fire a gun. I was uneasy at making any fire lest the smoke betray me.

I rejoiced at the discovery of a cave which went in a vast way. I resolved to bring hither some ammunition and stores, and persuaded myself that, if I hid there, five hundred savages could never find me.

My dog was a loving companion to me for most of my time, and then died of mere old age.

Spanish galleon
The Spanish ship spotted on the rocks by Crusoe was probably a three-masted Spanish galleon. These ships were used as warships or for trading for 300 years.

It was in the middle of May that it blew a great storm; and I was surprised with a noise of a gun fired at sea. I immediately considered this must be some ship in distress. When day broke I could plainly see the wreck. Its building was Spanish, jammed in between two rocks, all the stern and quarter beaten to pieces.

It was now calm, and I ventured out in my boat to this wreck. When I came close, a dog appeared and jumped into the sea to come to me. Besides the dog, there was nothing left on the ship that had life. What became of her crew I knew not. If only there had been but one soul saved, that I might have had one companion! Any goods that I could see were spoiled by the water, though I carried two seamen's chests into the boat. With this cargo, and the dog, I came away.

I got very little by this voyage that was any use to me. Besides some shirts, there were three bags of pieces of eight, six gold doubloons, and small bars of gold in the chests, but 'twas to me as the dirt under my feet.

Having secured all that I had gotten in my new cave, I made my way to my old habitation. For a while I lived easy enough; only I was more vigilant. If I did go abroad it was always to the east of the island, where I was well satisfied that savages never came. That is, until now.

Gold doubloons
The Spanish mined vast amounts of gold in Central and South America. It was made into coins, called doubloons, or into bars, and shipped back to Spain. Money is no use to Crusoe, so he pretends to despise it; yet he always squirrels away any that he finds.

I took two seamen's chests into the boat. With this cargo and the dog, I came away.

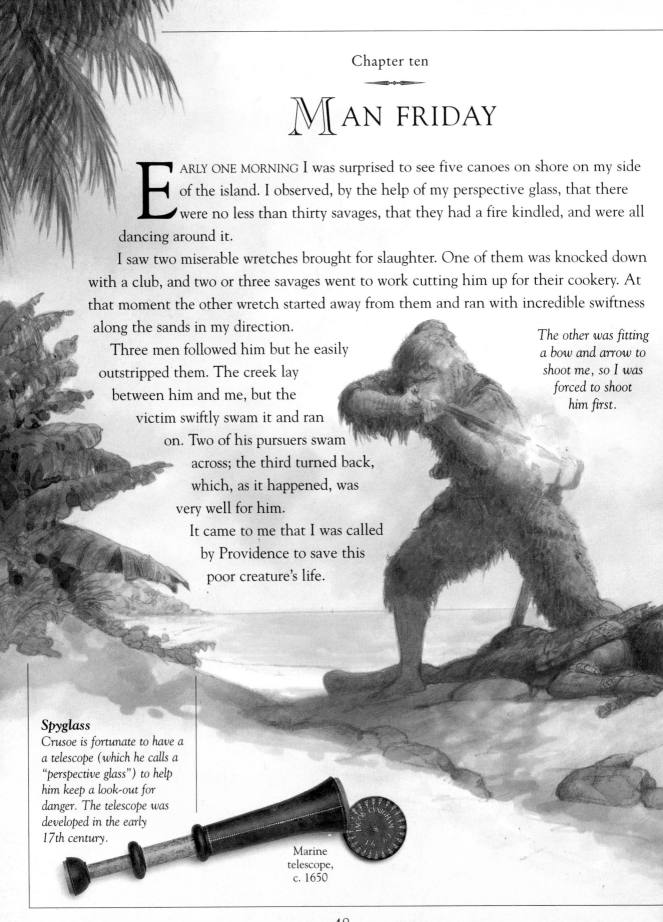

Chapter ten

Man Friday

EARLY ONE MORNING I was surprised to see five canoes on shore on my side of the island. I observed, by the help of my perspective glass, that there were no less than thirty savages, that they had a fire kindled, and were all dancing around it.

I saw two miserable wretches brought for slaughter. One of them was knocked down with a club, and two or three savages went to work cutting him up for their cookery. At that moment the other wretch started away from them and ran with incredible swiftness along the sands in my direction.

Three men followed him but he easily outstripped them. The creek lay between him and me, but the victim swiftly swam it and ran on. Two of his pursuers swam across; the third turned back, which, as it happened, was very well for him.

It came to me that I was called by Providence to save this poor creature's life.

The other was fitting a bow and arrow to shoot me, so I was forced to shoot him first.

Spyglass
Crusoe is fortunate to have a a telescope (which he calls a "perspective glass") to help him keep a look-out for danger. The telescope was developed in the early 17th century.

Marine telescope, c. 1650

I fetched my two guns and, taking a very short cut, descended to the shore and positioned myself between the two pursuers and the pursued. I advanced towards them; the foremost I knocked down with my gun; the other was fitting a bow and arrow to shoot me, so I was forced to shoot him first, and killed him. The poor savage who fled was so frightened by me, and with the fire and noise of my gun, that he stood stock still. I beckoned him with all the signs of encouragement I could think of. At length he came close to me, kneeled, and kissed the ground to thank me for saving his life.

I beckoned him to follow me. Upon this he signed that he should bury his pursuers, that they might not be seen. This being done, I took him to my cave. Here I gave him food and water and the poor wretch went to sleep.

The following day we went to where he had buried the two men. He made signs that we should dig them up and eat them; at this I made as if I would vomit at the thoughts of it.

In a little time I began to speak to him and teach him to speak to me. First I made him know his name, Friday, which was the day I saved his life.

A South American
Indian making arrows

Native weapons
The natives' bows and arrows were excellent for stealthy jungle hunting or warfare, but no match for Robinson Crusoe's gun on an open beach.

The conversation between Friday and I made the three years which we lived together perfectly happy.

I fell to work for my man Friday. I gave him a pair of linen drawers from the wreck; then I made him a jerkin of goatskin and a hareskin cap. I lodged him in a little tent between my two fortifications.

Never man had a more faithful servant than Friday was to me. I made it my business to teach him everything useful, but especially to speak English, and to understand me when I spoke to him. He was the aptest scholar.

The conversation between Friday and I made the three years which we lived together perfectly happy. He became a good Christian, a much better one than I, and told me he would never eat man's flesh any more.

He told me that there had been a great battle in which he had become a prisoner; and that it was the dreadful custom of the victors to bring prisoners taken in battle to this island, where they would kill and eat them.

Some time later, when we were standing on the hill at the west, from where I had first seen the mainland of America, Friday calls out to me: "O joy! O glad! There see my country!"

His extraordinary sense of pleasure told me that he longed to be in his own country again.

Venezuelan coast
The South American mainland that Friday calls his "country", is the coast of Venezuela. Columbus was the first European to land there, in 1498.

I went to work with Friday to make a large canoe.

I asked Friday a thousand questions about the mainland, and he told me all he knew, and that his people were Caribees. He said also that seventeen white men had been living with his people for about four years, since they were rescued from their boat. I suspected these might be the men escaped from the Spanish ship wrecked in sight of my island.

From this time I had a mind to venture with him to the mainland, and I went to work with Friday to make a large canoe to undertake the voyage.

I was now entered on the seven and twentieth year of my captivity and I had an invincible impression that I should not be another year in this place. I was preparing daily for the voyage and intended, in a week or a fortnight's time, to launch our boat.

A modern-day Carib craftsman

The Caribs
The Caribs (or "Caribees") come from the islands of the Lesser Antilles and the nearby South American coast. The islanders were once warlike and alleged to be cannibals. Those from the mainland, like Friday, were more peaceful. The Caribbean Sea is named after the Carib people.

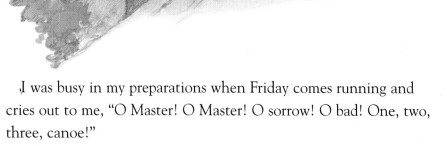

The poor fellow was most terribly scared that his enemies had come to look for him.

I was busy in my preparations when Friday comes running and cries out to me, "O Master! O Master! O sorrow! O bad! One, two, three, canoe!"

The poor fellow was most terribly scared that his enemies had come to look for him. I told him I was in as much danger as he.

"Friday," says I, "we must resolve to fight them."

I quickly discovered that there were one and twenty savages in the three canoes, and that they were landed near to my creek, where a thick wood came almost down to the sea. I gave Friday one pistol and three guns, and I took the same. With all possible wariness and silence, we marched till only one corner of the wood lay between me and them.

The savages were all around their fire, eating one of their prisoners. I was filled with horror when I saw a man, likely to be their next victim, lying bound upon the sand. Friday said he was one of the men that had come to their country in a boat. There was not a moment to lose.

"Now, Friday," said I, "do as I bid thee." With a musket, I took aim at the savages. "Then fire at them," said I.

They were in a dreadful consternation, for they knew not from whence their destruction came.

We fired again, then I rushed out of the wood, with Friday close behind me. I made directly towards the poor victim, while Friday fired on five who fled into a canoe. I cut him free, then asked him what countryman he was: he said "Spanish". I gave him a pistol and sword, and, as if they had put new vigour into him, he flew at his murderers like a fury.

The savages were so frightened by the noise of our guns, that they had no more power to escape than their flesh had to resist our shot.

In one of the canoes I found another poor prisoner, tied so tightly, neck and heels, that he had little life in him. Friday came up and embraced him, cried, laughed, danced, sang, then cried again. When he came a little to himself, he told me this man was his own father.

I made a hand-barrow, then Friday and I carried our new guests to my fortification, where I began making shelter and some provision for them.

The next day I ordered Friday to bury the dead. When I went there again, I could barely tell where the place of battle had been, other than by the corner of the wood pointing to the spot.

Pizarro slaughters the Incas

Spanish conquerors
The Spanish had been a powerful presence in the region ever since the 16th-century conquests of Pizarro and Cortez over the Inca and Aztec empires. Defoe was strongly critical of Spanish cruelty towards native South American cultures.

We fired again, then I rushed out of the wood, with Friday close behind me.

Chapter eleven

THE MUTINEERS

Mutineers, led by Fletcher Christian, cast the *Bounty's* commander, Lieutenant Bligh, and several others adrift.

Mutiny on board ship

Bad food or brutal treatment were the usual reasons for a ship's crew to mutiny, though the mutineers in this episode seem to have no valid motives. The most famous mutiny in British naval history remains the mutiny on HMS Bounty of 1789.

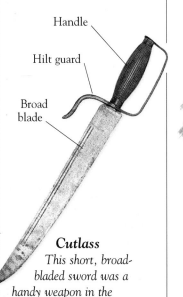

Handle

Hilt guard

Broad blade

Cutlass

This short, broad-bladed sword was a handy weapon in the confined spaces of a ship. It was much-used by seamen and was ideal for slashing and cutting.

M Y ISLAND was now peopled and I began to enter into conversation with my two new subjects. In conversation with the Spaniard, I learned that there were sixteen more of his countrymen who, their ship having been wrecked, had made their escape to the mainland. I proposed that if they were all brought here, to my island, we might, with so many hands, build a ship to carry us all away, either to the Brazils southward, or to the Spanish coast northward.

The Spaniard answered that, if I pleased, he would go to them with Friday's father and speak with them and bring me their answer. Under this agreement they left in one of the canoes that they were brought in. I gave them each a musket and provisions for many days.

I had waited no less than eight days, when a strange and unforeseen accident intervened. Instead of the return of the canoe, I saw what appeared to be an English ship, lying at anchor. Yet some secret doubts hung about me, bidding me keep upon my guard.

I observed a long boat come on shore. There were in all eleven men, whereof three were bound as prisoners. I saw one villain lift up a great cutlass and I stood trembling with horror, expecting the three would be killed.

The poor distressed prisoners were set down and looked like men in despair. When I observed the seamen were all gone into the woods, and, as I thought, were laid down to sleep. I came with Friday as near to the prisoners as I could.

"Gentlemen," said I, "pray lay aside your fears. I am an Englishman, and disposed to assist you."

"Sir," said one of the men, "I was commander of that ship. My men have mutinied against me and have set us on shore, where we expect to perish."

He gave me assurances that if we were to assist him to recover his ship, he would carry me and my man to England.

"Well then," said I, "here are three muskets for you; tell me next what you think is proper to be done."

Punishable by death
Mutiny was regarded as a terrible crime by the authorities, and the penalty for it was death. Unless a mutineer had influential friends, he was unlikely to escape the gallows, if caught.

I came, with Friday, as near to the prisoners as I could.

About midnight, the captain ventured, with twelve hands, on board the ship.

Boatswains were known as strict disciplinarians – as this 19th-century caricature by George Cruikshank shows.

Position of power
One of the ringleaders of the mutiny, the boatswain, was an important officer on board the ship. He was responsible for the sails, rigging, and other equipment.

My comrades fell upon their captors. They shot two before the rest saw their danger. The captain told them he would spare them their lives if they would swear to be faithful to him. This they solemnly promised to do.

Our business was now to recapture the ship. There were still six and twenty hands on board. The captain feared that they might set sail, giving up their comrades for lost, but in a little while, ten of the ship's crew, wondering what had become of their comrades, hoisted another boat out and rowed towards the shore. On landing, the men left only two with their boat while they searched for their missing comrades in the woods. We surprised these two men, persuaded them to join us, and lay in wait for the rest.

On their return from the woods, dejected and dispirited, we came upon them in the dark. The boatswain, who was a ringleader, was killed on the spot. At this, they all laid down their arms, begged for their lives, and promised to join in an attempt to recapture the ship.

About midnight, while I and Friday stayed to guard the remaining prisoners, the captain and twelve hands ventured on board the ship. After they had secured the decks, the captain ordered three men to

break into the roundhouse where the rebel captain lay. During an exchange of fire he was shot through the head, upon which the rest surrendered without any more lives being lost.

Seven guns were fired to give notice of this success, which I was glad to hear, having sat watching upon the shore till near two in the morning. I laid me down and slept very soundly.

I awoke when I heard the captain's voice; there he stood, and pointing to the ship, he embraced me in his arms. "My dear friend," says he, "there's your ship, for she is all yours."

I was not able to answer him; but as he had taken me in his arms, I held fast, otherwise I would have fallen to the ground.

Such was the flood of joy in my heart that it put all my sprits into confusion. I looked upon him as a man sent from heaven to save me.

"My dear friend," says he, "there's your ship, for she is all yours."

🌴
The roundhouse
This was a semi-circular cabin at the stern of the ship. It was situated on the quarter deck, which was where the officers lived.

A marooned pirate contemplates a bleak future

Left to rot
It was a common punishment, particularly among pirates, to maroon wrongdoers on desert islands. Here the mutineers prefer being marooned to being hanged in England.

James II, by Samuel Cooper

Changing times
Crusoe has been away from England for some 35 years, so it is not surprising he feels a total stranger. When he left, the country was ruled by Oliver Cromwell; now England is once again a monarchy, with James II on the throne.

Chapter twelve

A PERFECT STRANGER

I LEFT THE ISLAND on the 19 December, in the year 1686, after I had been upon it eight and twenty years, two months and nineteen days. My man Friday accompanied me, and proved a most faithful servant. I also carried with me my goat's-skin cap, my umbrella, and my parrot; also I did not forget the money which had been useless to me for so long that it had grown rusty or tarnished.

Three of the most incorrigible rogues decided to take their fate on the island rather than return to England in irons, be tried for mutiny, and risk the gallows. I left them some firearms and instructions as to how they could live quite comfortably. I also told them that the Spaniards and Friday's father would someday arrive from the mainland and I made them promise to treat them well.

When I came to England, I was a perfect stranger to all the world, as I had been long given over for dead. My father and mother had long since died, and left me nothing in their wills.

I enquired after my plantation in the Brazils and was told that my partner had grown exceedingly rich from just one half of it. Accordingly, I sold my half share in the plantation for 33,000 pieces of eight.

I settled in the Brazils, married, had three children, two sons and one daughter, and left off all thoughts of wandering. But when my wife, the centre of all my enterprises, died, I longed to see my island, and to know if the poor Spaniards were there, and how the three English rogues I left behind had treated them.

At last, in the year 1694, I visited my island again. I met the Spaniard and many of his countrymen, and Friday saw his father once again. I stayed about twenty days, left them supplies of all necessary things, and heard the whole story of their lives. All these things, with some very surprising incidents in some new adventures of my own I may perhaps give a farther account of hereafter.

When I came to England, I was a perfect stranger to all the world, as I had been long given over for dead.

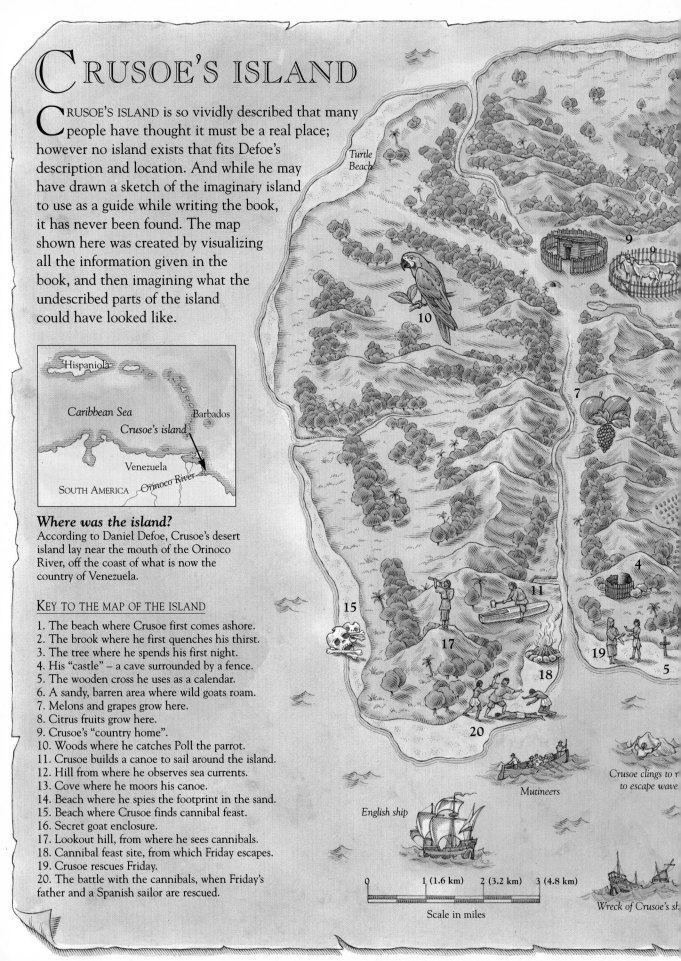

CRUSOE'S ISLAND

CRUSOE'S ISLAND is so vividly described that many people have thought it must be a real place; however no island exists that fits Defoe's description and location. And while he may have drawn a sketch of the imaginary island to use as a guide while writing the book, it has never been found. The map shown here was created by visualizing all the information given in the book, and then imagining what the undescribed parts of the island could have looked like.

Where was the island?
According to Daniel Defoe, Crusoe's desert island lay near the mouth of the Orinoco River, off the coast of what is now the country of Venezuela.

KEY TO THE MAP OF THE ISLAND

1. The beach where Crusoe first comes ashore.
2. The brook where he first quenches his thirst.
3. The tree where he spends his first night.
4. His "castle" – a cave surrounded by a fence.
5. The wooden cross he uses as a calendar.
6. A sandy, barren area where wild goats roam.
7. Melons and grapes grow here.
8. Citrus fruits grow here.
9. Crusoe's "country home".
10. Woods where he catches Poll the parrot.
11. Crusoe builds a canoe to sail around the island.
12. Hill from where he observes sea currents.
13. Cove where he moors his canoe.
14. Beach where he spies the footprint in the sand.
15. Beach where Crusoe finds cannibal feast.
16. Secret goat enclosure.
17. Lookout hill, from where he sees cannibals.
18. Cannibal feast site, from which Friday escapes.
19. Crusoe rescues Friday.
20. The battle with the cannibals, when Friday's father and a Spanish sailor are rescued.

Turtle Beach

Hispaniola

Caribbean Sea

Barbados

Crusoe's island

Venezuela

SOUTH AMERICA   Orinoco River

Mutineers

English ship

Crusoe clings to r
to escape wave

Wreck of Crusoe's sh

0   1 (1.6 km)   2 (3.2 km)   3 (4.8 km)

Scale in miles

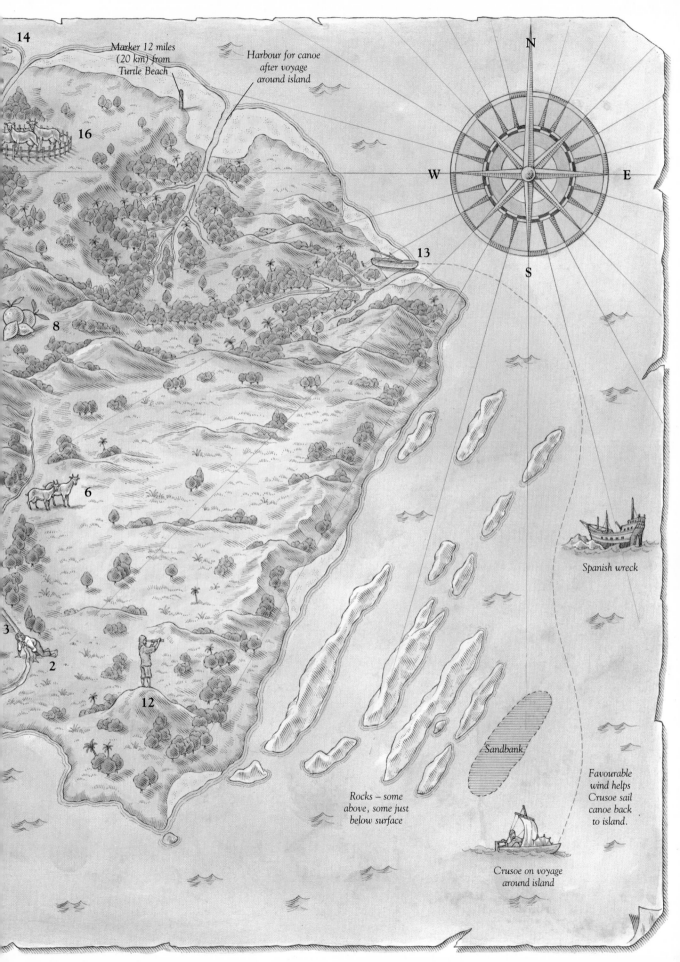

14

*Marker 12 miles
(20 km) from
Turtle Beach*

*Harbour for canoe
after voyage
around island*

16

N

W   **E**

13

S

8

6

3

2

12

Spanish wreck

Sandbank

*Rocks – some
above, some just
below surface*

*Favourable
wind helps
Crusoe sail
canoe back
to island.*

*Crusoe on voyage
around island*

DEFOE'S ADVENTURES

LIKE HIS MOST famous character, Robinson Crusoe, Daniel Defoe was an outsider all his life. He took part in a disastrous rebellion against the British Crown, endured numerous business failures, and became a controversial journalist. He was then imprisoned for his political and religious views, and worked as a government spy. He also spent much of his life in debt and on the run from creditors. Yet though he achieved little success in his lifetime, his books are now world-famous.

DANIEL DEFOE: KEY DATES

1660: Born in London.
1684: Marries wife, Mary.
1685: Joins the Duke of Monmouth's rebellion.
1692: Imprisoned for debt, after several business failures; becomes a journalist.
1703: Imprisoned for criticizing the Church of England.
1704: Released from prison.
1704-1713: Works as a controversial political journalist, and as a government spy.
1714-25: Career as novelist.
1719: *Robinson Crusoe* published.
1731: Dies alone in London, deep in debt.

Money worries

Defoe used his wife's money to set himself up as a merchant. However, after the failure of various get-rich-quick schemes, he was thrown into the Fleet prison for debt.

THE WORKS OF DANIEL DEFOE

For many years Daniel Defoe was a prolific and influential journalist, producing his own newspaper. He began writing fiction late in life – his first novel, Robinson Crusoe, *was published in 1719, when he was 59. It brought him instant fame.*

Following Crusoe

Defoe followed up his first novel with two sequels, *The Farther Adventures of Robinson Crusoe* (1719) and *The Serious Reflections of Robinson Crusoe* (1720). Neither one was a hit with the public. They were followed by the more popular *Moll Flanders* (1722), in which he drew upon his own experiences of being imprisoned, *A Journal of the Plague Year* (1722), and *Roxana* (1724). His non-fictional works include *A Tour Through the Whole Island of Great Britain* (1726).

Sedgmoor

In 1685 Defoe took part in the Duke of Monmouth's rebellion against the new king, the Catholic James II. Defoe was on the losing side at the Battle of Sedgemoor, but escaped. Many of the Duke's followers were hanged.

The Battle of Sedgemoor

Religious turmoil

Throughout the 17th century England was divided by religion. Some people disagreed with the form of worship in the Church of England. They were called Dissenters, and Defoe was one of them. The Dissenters – strict Protestants – feared that a Catholic king would persecute them for their beliefs.

Defoe in the pillory

Dissenters, like these Quakers, used to meet in private houses.

Man of principle

Defoe believed passionately in freedom of worship for all and campaigned for his principles in articles and pamphlets. In 1703 he was imprisoned and put in the pillory for his criticism of the government and the church. He was lucky to survive.

Rescued by royalty

The Speaker of the House of Commons, Robert Harley, persuaded Queen Anne to pay Defoe's fine and free him from prison. She also sent money to his wife and six children. Harley was head of the Secret Service. He persuaded Defoe to become a spy and sent him around the country to find out what enemies of the government were thinking.

Anne, Queen of Britain from 1702–14, by William Wissing.

A lonely death

The tragic final days of the famous author were spent hiding from creditors in lodgings in the City of London, too fearful of arrest to even see his family.

This monument was put up in north London by The Christian World newspaper in 1870.

CRUSOE'S CONTINUING ADVENTURES

With the pace of modern life increasing with every decade, Defoe's resourceful hero, stranded far away from crowds, traffic chaos, and pollution, has retained enormous appeal. Real-life adventurers have tried living like Crusoe themselves, and the story has been adapted for the screen several times. It has even been given a sci-fi setting, in which Robinson Crusoe is cast away in Outer Space.

THE MOST FABULOUS HERO IN ALL ADVENTURE HISTORY!

ADVENTURES OF ROBINSON CRUSOE

DANIEL DEFOE's Immortal Classic

COLOUR BY PATHECOLOR

Starring DAN O'HERLIHY with JAMES FERNANDEZ

Produced by Oscar DANCIGERS and HENRY EHRLICH Directed by Luis BUNUEL

Castaway

In this 1986 film, based on the bestselling true account by Lucy Irvine, a man advertises for a "Girl Friday" to go adventuring with on a desert island like Robinson Crusoe.

Spaceman Crusoe rescues Man Friday from warlike aliens in Robinson Crusoe on Mars.

True to the book

Made in 1953 by the Spanish director Luis Bunuel, *The Adventures of Robinson Crusoe* superbly evoked the atmosphere of the original novel.

Life on Mars

The sci-fi movie, *Robinson Crusoe on Mars* (1964) showed that the story could work surprisingly well without a beach or palm tree in sight.

Acknowledgements

Picture Credits

The publishers would like to thank the following for their kind permission to reproduce their photographs:

a = above; c = centre; b = below/bottom;
l = left; r = right; t = top.

AKG London: 20 cl, 22 cl, 45, 53.
Bridgeman Art Library, London/New York: British Library, London: *Jonah and the Whale*, detail from p.347-8 (Terra Sancta) Mercator's "Atlas...", 1619 11 tr; Christie's Images: *The Shipwreck*, 1873 by Ivan Konstaniovich Aivazovsky (1817-1900) (attr. to) 16 tl; Museum Boymans, van Beuningen, Rotterdam: *Lawyer in his Study* by Adrian Jansz van Ostade (1610-85) 8 cl; National Maritime Museum, London: *The Mutineers Casting Bligh Adrift in the Launch*, 1789, engraving by Robert Dodd 54 tl; Private Collection: *The Capture of Pirate Blackbeard*, 1718 by Jean Leon Jerome Ferris (1863-1930) 17 cbr; Royal Geographical Society, London: World Map: "*Nova Totius Terrarum Orbis Geographica Ac Hydrographica Tabula*", 1608, based on Columbus' Voyage of 1492, by Pieter Van Den Keere, and pub. by Jan Jansonn (1596-1664) c.1650 2, 6-7; Scottish National Portrait Gallery, Edinburgh: *Queen Anne (1665-1714)* by William Wissing or Wissmig (1656-87) 63 tc; Victoria & Albert Museum: *The Bradford Table Carpet*, detail of men fishing and duck shooting, embroidered on linen canvas in coloured silks, English, late 16th century 35; William Clements Library, University of Michigan: *The Massacre of Indians at Cholula on the orders of Cortez*, 1519 (w/c) 6 clb;
© Trustees of the British Museum: 7 tc, ca, 25 crb.
J. Allan Cash Ltd: 14 tl.
Christie's Images: 7 b; Guariento di Arpo 31.
Bruce Coleman Ltd: Staffan Widstrand 33 br.
Delaware Art Museum: Howard Pyle Collection, Museum purchase, 1912 5.
Mary Evans Picture Library: 7 cbr, 33 tr, 43 t, 62 cr, cbr; T. M. Gregory, The Gregory Collection 23 cr.
ET Archive: 62 bc.
Exeter Maritime Museum: 38.
Hulton Getty: 8 tl, 9 tr, 17 tr, 56, 62 tl.
The Ronald Grant Archive: *Castaway* © Cannon 63 cr; *1492: The Conquest of Paradise* © Guild Distribution 6 tl; *Adventures of Robinson Crusoe* © Universal 63 cl.
Katz Pictures Ltd: The Mansell Collection 7 c.
Frank Lane Picture Agency: American Red Cross 29.
London Library: from George Lee's *Daniel Defoe: His Life and Hitherto Unknown Writings* 62 bl.
Moviestore Collection: *The Bounty* © Bounty 17 cr; *Robinson Crusoe on Mars* © Paramount Pictures 63 b.
Museum of London: 17 br.
National Maritime Museum Picture Library: 16 cbr, br, 58 bl.
National Maritime Museum, London: 6 br, 16 cl, cbl, 17 bl, 18 cl, 23 tr, cr, 46, 47, 48, 54 bl.
Natural History Museum, London: 44.
Panos Pictures: John Miles 49.
Robert Harding Picture Library: Jeremy Bright 43 b.
South American Pictures: Tony Morrison 17 tl, 39, 50, 51.
St Malo Museum: 12 bl.
Telegraph Colour Library: Bavaria-Bildagentur 21 tr; Paul Campbell 11 cr.
Tanya Tween: 63 tr.
Victoria & Albert Museum: 34.

Jacket: **Bridgeman Art Library, London/New York:** Royal Geographical Society, London: World Map: "*Nova Totius Terrarum Orbis Geographica Ac Hydrographica Tabula*", 1608, based on Columbus' Voyage of 1492, by Pieter Van Den Keere, and pub. by Jan Jansonn (1596-1664) c.1650 back tl.
Hulton Getty: inside back.
National Maritime Museum, London: front tl, trt, trb, cl, back tr, c, bc.
St Malo Museum: back cla.
Victoria & Albert Museum: back clb.

Additional illustrations: Sallie Alane Reason; John Woodcock; Stephen Raw.

Additional photography: Dave King; Chas Howson; James Stevenson; Tina Chambers; Steve Gorton; Roger Philips; Philip Dowell; Andy Crawford.

Dorling Kindersley would particularly like to thank the following people:

Marie Greenwood and Nick Turpin for proof-reading; James Dunbar and Kate Joyce for researching the map of Crusoe's Island.